The Last Bridge

Some lines are drawn in ink. Others are drawn in blood.

First Edition

Written By: Ronan Valehart

Published By: AmeraVinci Press

The Last Bridge

Published by: AmeraVinci Press
ISBN (Paperback Edition): 979-8-9999263-1-9

An Imprint of AmeraVinci Venture, LLC
For those who believe every story has a place in the world

Table Of Contents

Dedication

To my family, by blood and by bond:
To those who stood by me, loved me, challenged me, and lifted me up when I stumbled; I am blessed beyond measure to call you family. This is as much yours as it is mine.

To the Men, Women, and Airmen of the Intrepid Spirit Center, 96th Medical Group, Eglin Air Force Base:
Your tireless dedication to serving those who have served, and your unwavering commitment to guiding service members through the hidden battles of TBI, have given many of us the tools to find our way out of the dark. You reminded me that no one has to fight alone, and you helped me discover that creativity can be a weapon of hope.

To the extraordinary staff of the Fisher House at Eglin Air Force Base:
Thank you for your selfless service, your quiet acts of kindness, and the love you extend to every warrior and family who walks through your doors. In those walls, I found not only a place to heal, but the space to bring these words to life.

To AmeraVinci:
For believing in stories, in possibility, and in the people who dare to create them. Your faith turned an idea into

something real, and your family first spirit reminds us that the right support can turn visions into victories. May the stories you help bring into the world continue to bear your mark, for those who know where to look.

To all service members that is past, present, and future:
Who give their everything, often at a cost far greater than most will ever know. Your courage, sacrifice, and steadfast will are the bridges the rest of us walk across.

And lastly this is for:
Every parent who has stood between danger and their family.
Every soldier who has drawn the line and never stepped back.
Every person who has stood over to protect those who have fallen.

Your stance will be remembered.
Your sacrifice will not be forgotten.
Your love will carry on.

Chapter One: The Weight of Quiet

When peace is rare, it is carried like a prayer.

The house breathed.

It was not alive, not in the way flesh was, but it pulsed gently in the morning light, as if remembering it had once been something more than timber and stone.

Sunlight slanted through the oversized window frame, scattering dappled rays across the hard slate floor. The shutters had been propped open, and the breeze carried the scent of warm broth and ground herbs through the room. It smelled like a memory. It smelled like peace.

A girl, ten years old perhaps, stood on a crate at the thick wood table. Her hands were small but sure. The blade she handled was longer than her forearm, but that did not matter. She used it with ease, rhythmically slicing vegetables into neat piles. Her humming was low, tuneless, almost imperceptible, a sound not meant for others but for herself.

Her clothes were oversized, pale off white, smudged in flour and herbs. The shirt billowed when she moved. She did not notice the size, or the weight of the blade. She simply worked.

Her mother stood beside her.

Quiet. Watchful.

She stirred a pot that rested on a glowing metal disc, technology half buried in the room's rustic bones. She was lean, built for work. Her arms were wiry, not soft. Her braid was thick, dark, and hung low. Her face was worn but not tired. There was a kind of strength behind her hazel eyes, focused and steady, the kind of strength that bent for nothing but love.

She smiled, just barely.

The boy at the far table did not seem to notice. He was too busy with his sketchpad. Elbows anchored, shoulders slightly hunched, pencil moving in short, decisive strokes. He was older than the girl, fourteen perhaps. His dark, unkempt hair fell into his eyes. He brushed it away absently, repeatedly, never looking up for long.

His art was not scribbling. It was structure. Precision. Curved lines with internal logic, like he had studied more than paper and ink.

Near the hearth, nestled into a worn loveseat with a sag in its frame, the Eldest daughter worked her needle. She was maybe nineteen. Dark hair, up in a tight bun. A uniform, because that was what it resembled, was folded across her lap, half finished. Not armor. Not clothing. Something else. Stitched with black leather, reinforced fabric, and intent.

Her fingers moved with machine regularity, never pausing. She was not distracted. Just silent. Like she belonged to a different time than the room around her. One more thread. One more stitch. One more breath of peace.

In the corner, shadowed but not hidden, sat the Father.

The man was still. A relaxed stillness. Not sleep. Not laziness. Just readiness.

Broad shoulders. Old scars. A red shirt fraying at the seams. Sweatpants that had seen more use than the furniture. His chair creaked beneath him, one arm draped across the tabletop. The monitor beside him cast a faint blue hue on one side of his face. Sunlight struck the other.

Two lights. Two lives.

His pale blue eyes, scarred at the corners, scanned the room. Not for threat. Not today. He simply watched. This was his unit. His fire team. His family.
And for a moment, one long, beautiful, crushing moment, they were safe.

He closed his eyes and exhaled.

Not the sigh of someone escaping pain, but the exhale of someone holding onto something they knew they would not have for long.

He did not speak.

None of them did.

There was no need.

The morning held its breath.

And the house remembered.

Chapter Two: Protocol Red

When peace can end in the space between heartbeats.

The monitor changed.

No sound. No alarm. No voice.
Just light.

The soft blue hue that had lit the Father's face for the last hour pulsed once, then again, red. Deep. Urgent. Rhythmic.

He did not blink. He did not shift.

But something behind his eyes changed.

His shoulders squared by a fraction of a degree. The faint line at the corner of his mouth, the one that had been a smile, disappeared. His hand, once relaxed, curled slowly around the edge of the table.

He looked to her first. Always to her.

His wife. Still at the pot. Still stirring. Still at ease. But not for long.

She felt it.

Her head came up sharply. Not violent, not panicked, but precise. She saw him. Saw the change. And she knew.

Spoon down.

Not dropped. Placed.

It made a soft wooden clack against the tables top. A sound no louder than a heartbeat.

She was already moving.

The Eldest on the loveseat looked up next. She had not been spoken to. No signal. No orders. But she saw the motion, read the lines on her mother's face, and understood.

She folded the piece of cloth she had been sewing on, set it down beside her like it mattered, like it still had time to become something. The needle remained threaded, looped through the half-stitched seam.

Standing, taking the folded uniform with her.

No wasted motion.

The boy lifted his eyes from his sketchpad as if instinct had triggered him, not noise. He followed his sister's movement, then his mother's path.

Then his father.

And that was enough.

He slid the pencil into the spine of the sketchpad, closed it without slamming, and stood.

Even the little one, the girl on the crate, humming as she cut, stopped. Not because anyone said anything, but because suddenly the room was in motion, all of them moving.

She looked around. Her brother. Her sister. Her mother.

Her Father, still sitting, but the hardened look was back on his face.

No panic.

Just silence filled with purpose.

She stepped off the crate. Her boots tapped twice on the stone. Quiet. Measured.

And like that, the room moved as one.

They became a team. No longer just a family at breakfast, in a peaceful room.

A formation.

The boy turned from his sketch table. Crossed the room to an old chest. Sitting against the north wall near the hearth. The latch clicked once, clean.

The Mother crossed the room in twelve steps. Three chests sat in the corner of the west wall. Her fingers did not hesitate on the center one. The lid rose.

The Eldest moved to her own chest, just to the left of her mother. One knee down, hand already lifting the lid. The Youngest followed, kneeling to the right of her mother, like it was a routine drill.

Two zones of operation.

Four operators opened their chests.

Latches clicked. Hinges creaked. Their gear now exposed.

The Father had not moved.

Not until now.

Then he stood, slowly, like the moment itself needed permission to escalate.

The Last Bridge

He turned to the chest near his seat. A simple drop to one knee. The lid opened without a sound.

Zone three active. The fifth and last operator open his chest.

He had no need to look in.

Everything in there was hard burnt muscle memory.

Opening this was far from his first time.

Chapter Three: A Darker Nature
When the forest stops breathing...run!

The forest held its breath.

Sunlight filtered through the trees in thin strands, but it felt wrong, like the light had been stretched too far, too thin. The leaves did not rustle. The air did not move. Even the birds were silent.

Then, motion.

A rustle. Distant. Wrong.

Not a breeze.

Footsteps.

Too many. Too fast.

A shape burst through the tree line, then another. Black fur. Gnarled limbs. Massive paws pounded the soil, displacing moss and loose earth with every leap. Fangs bared. Eyes glowing. Saliva hanging in ropes from their jaws.

They ran low. Fast. Silent.

Hellhounds.

Not animals. Not even monsters.

Cruel designs of death.

Creatures molded in violence. Scar twisted flesh stretched over long, unnatural bones. Faces shaped into something wolf like, but leaner. Hungrier. Bred for blood.

One stopped.

Sniffed.

Another followed. Then a third.

Then, silence again.

And something worse behind it.

Something upright.

Something humanoid.

Barely.

It darted through the underbrush like a shadow, sleek black skin catching the light for half a second before vanishing again. One clawed hand braced against a tree, carving deep ruts into the bark with no effort at all.

Its head followed.

Bat like. Elongated. Eyes of pure black evil.

A single, rupturing wail, low at first, then climbing to a frequency that shattered the calm like a dropped blade in a quiet church.

More followed.

They did not emerge. They spilled.

Six feet tall. Spines bristling with spikes. Limbs segmented and bent wrong. Hands ending in cruel tools. Stubs where tails should be. Some with extra rage. Some with nothing but hunger.

Demon Warriors.

Not beasts.

Weapons, built to be soldiers.

Manufactured in some dark pit where flesh was currency and pain was a blueprint.

Dozens surged forward, Demon Warriors and Hellhounds in a synchronized sprint, barely touching the forest floor. Their speed was inhuman. Their silence worse.

Then the tremors began.

Different cadence. Slower. Heavier.

A second rhythm.

The trees swayed, not with wind, but pressure.

Branches cracked.

Brush collapsed.

Something massive moved behind the pack.

A Brute.

Eight feet tall. Fire charred skin. Armor strapped together with bone and metal scraps. Eyes like dead coals behind a face that had forgotten what symmetry was. It did not carry, it dragged, a slab of black steel trailed from one hand, not shaped like a sword, but like a piece of building torn out.

It was not a weapon.

It was a promise.

More Brutes followed, breaking trees without flinching, jaws slack, muscles twitching beneath hides of scarred meat and twisted metal.

Behind them, more.

An army.

A tide.

A horde of Hellhounds, Demon Warriors, and Brutes.

And something else behind it all.

Watching.

Waiting.

The edge of the woods crackled cold with their presence. The light receded. Midmorning haze gave way to something dusk like. It was a light that did not belong to this time of day at all. It was trying to hide or was being chased away.

And in the distance, cradled on a rise just before the cliffs, a worn white stone large building stood untouched.

Still.

The Last Bridge

Unaware.

A lie waiting to be broken.

One Demon Warrior halted at the tree line. It lifted a blade like finger dripping. It's point in line with the cozy building.

Its jaw split open letting out a scream, low and slow, a terrifying alert. A signal.

The horde paused.

Then moved as one.

With a destination found.

Faster now.

As if death had remembered it was behind schedule.

Chapter Four: Formation
When family becomes more than a target.

The room moved like muscle memory.

They were not soldiers in uniform. Not yet. But the shift was unmistakable.

No more morning light. No more humming. No more food, thread, sketches, or warmth.

This was protocol.

The Mother removing from her opened chest first.

Black and purple rippled in the air, her suit. Full-body. Seamless. Reinforced with matte-black plating that hugged her frame as if it had been grown, not fabricated. She stepped into it under her dress, drawing it up in one practiced motion. The fabric sealed with a low hiss.

Armor came next.

Carbon fiber chest harness. Dual buckles, one at the clavicle, one at the hip. Straps adjusted without thought.
Her hands moved along the rows of gear: trauma shears, comms node, reloads, check, check, check.

The Last Bridge

She drew the rifle last. Compact. Battleworn. It hummed faintly as it came online. Familiar weight. No hesitation. Bolt checked. Chamber clear. Sling adjusted.

A short katana slid into a magnetized sheath on her hip.

No words.

Next to her, the Youngest knelt by her own chest. Already in uniform. Faded pink camo over black, faded and worn in, not for fashion, but legacy. She ran her hands over a trauma pack the size of her torso, checking vials, injectors, and surgical sealant. Nothing dramatic.

She lifted a warn photo of the family. They are together peacefully and smiling, even her Father.
Without a word, she slid it into a pouch and zipped it shut.
A pistol clicked into place on her thigh. Magnetized. Locked.

Across the room, the Son geared up, his motions slightly faster. Not panicked. Just practiced. His matte grey suit sealed up the spine, sleeves locking down over reinforced arm guards.

A drop leg holster secured to his thigh. A blade across his back. Not decorative. Full-length. Designed to draw on the pivot.

His body armor was layered over the top, old leather straps interwoven with modern buckles. He clipped a drum to his squad automatic weapon, known as a SAW, from the crate, charged it, then tapped a small panel. A low whine vibrated through the weapon. Blue lines pulsed along the receiver.

It was ready.

And so was he.

The Eldest had not spoken. Her chest opened like the others, silent as breath. Her uniform was deep blue, trimmed in ink-black, tight like a second skin. Her chest rig was compact, loaded with long, stubby magazines.

Her hands were precise.

Gloves on. Right trigger finger exposed.

She pulled the neck of her black uniform up over her face, just past the bridge of her nose. Only her eyes remained visible. Calm. Alert.

From her case, she drew a long sniper rifle. The matte finish, scratched to hell. The scope longer than most carbines. She slid the magazine in. Locked it. Tapped the side. The rifle pulsed once, alive.

Each step, flawless.

Across the room, the Father stood done. Waiting.

His armor was black. No decals. No ornament. Just war torn plating, scarred down the center of the chest from a blade that had not finished the job. His gloves were fingerless at the thumb, trigger, and middle, dexterity over protection.
Weapons lined his frame.

Two swords on his left hip. Pistol at his right. Another across his chest for cross draw. Twin knives across the lower back. Balanced. Accessible.

He stood in front of them now, not a man, but a wall. A center point.

They faced him in formation.

Left to right: The Eldest, the Son, the Youngest, then the Mother.

Perfectly spaced.

No salutes. No slogans. No bravado.

Only readiness and purpose.

A legacy standing together.

He looked at each of them. Not to inspect.

With pride and approval.

Then he nodded once to his eldest.

She turned. Pealing off, as the others followed.

A hallway on the west wall waited, just beyond an open door.

She vanished into it. Enveloped by a blue hue of light.

One by one, lost down the open door.

No orders. No words.

Just execution.

And behind them, the man who had made them into this.

Paused last. Looking over the room.

From the window. The morning light was slowly pulling back. It too was going to safety.

The hallway swallowed him in a soft blue and a short red pulse of light.

The Last Bridge

He pulled the heavy door shut behind him and locked it with a steel bar.

Chapter Five: First Contact

When the hunt catches your scent.

The door on the east wall in the south corner exploded. The iron bar, once bound to oak, blasted inward. A moment ago, a large menacing door, now bits of shrapnel sliding across the stone.

A slab of black steel cleaved the thick door in a single blow, crashing to the floor with a shower of sparks.

Its mangled edge, shaped like some massive blade or twisted piece of steel. It clanged through the opening, then began to slide back into the shadow from which it came.

The sound of dragging metal scraped over wood and stone… drowned out by a howl.

A long, deep, crackling howl, too heavy and too long to belong to anything natural, rolled through the chamber.

The first Hellhound burst through the breach before the massive steel cleaver had even cleared.

It hit the room like a fired projectile, claws gouging the floor, eyes burning, searching for movement, wanting desperately to lock on, so it could launch into pure destruction.

A second followed, not charging blindly but with intent.

It bounded in great, arcing leaps to the far corner and landed on the Father's now empty chair, jaws crushing the frame into splinters.

Its snarls of frustration echoed off the stone.

Its need to hunt is not out of hunger.

But to desecrate and destroy.

A child's small cloth doll lay on the floor.

The Hellhound snatched it up, shook it until the seams tore and the stuffing spilled out, then dropped it. Shredded, wet and limp.

An empty victory to feed its endless rage.

The pot, still warm. The stew inside slowly spills out steam.

A spoon quietly resting where it had been placed.

A book, closed with care, lay on a small table.

A loveseat still held the warmth of the body it was holding in its embrace. A piece of cloth lay patiently draped over its arm, waiting to be finished.

Chests lay open, contents stripped.

This was no longer a home.

It was a hollowed out shell. Left for them, emptied of everything that mattered.

They had taken only what they needed.

Themselves.

Four Demon Warriors slithered through the threshold behind the Hellhounds, black skinned, bone thin frames, clawed fingers dripping twitching like broken, venomous insects.

Mouths always open. No breath. No words.

Just readiness. Their heads swiveled, black eyes scanning high and low for their target.

They crouched as they moved, measuring each step, ready to spring the moment they found a sign.

A Brute came last, smashing the remainder of the door and frame with one massive fist.

It hunched as it forced itself through, dragging its cleaver sized blade across the stone, gouging a deep scar in the floor.

Shoulder armor scraped the frame. Blood, both dried and fresh, crusted its jawline.

It was far too large for the space, cracking stone and raking wooden ceiling beams as it moved. It didn't care.

The random wooden furniture slid out of its way or was crushed and splintered. Anything in its path was meaningless. It was a living wrecking ball searching for what had been there and obliterating everything that was left behind.

The Demon Warriors prowled through the space, stabbing with needle length claws at left behind items, calculating, searching for the faintest clue.

The Hellhounds paced in tightening circles, nostrils flaring, amped on the overwhelming scent of their prey that clung to every surface.

They needed something to tear into.

Something malleable.

Something alive.

But there was nothing left.

They were already gone.

But gone didn't mean safe. The scent still clung to stone, to air, to memory. And the hunt was on the move, just on the other side of that closed door in the corner of the room.

Chapter Six: Pursuit

When the distance closes faster than you can escape.

The narrow arched stone hallway stretched ahead, the cobblestone wall split by a single blue strip of light running its length along the midline.

Above, heavy stone arches broke the low ceiling into measured intervals. Between them, narrow fixtures pulsed with a slow, deliberate red glow, each beat casting the corridor in a brief wash of ominous light.

The cool, steady blue kept the place in a calm half sleep. The red was its heartbeat. Slow. Methodical. Waiting. Warning.

The hallway burst to life.

The Eldest rounded the corner first, silent as a passing draft. Her sniper rifle tight across the back, a sword hilt jutting over her opposite shoulder. Her steps were swift and certain, no fear, only speed.

Her brother followed close, SAW slung across his chest, an ammunition belt taut. Every footfall gave a whisper of a metallic chank, every other step in sync with the red pulse above, like the hallway itself was keeping pace.

The Youngest trailed, light and quick, one hand clamped to her pack strap to keep it from bouncing. Her boots tapped a soft rhythm over the stone, her breath steady.

The Mother came next, as a ghost given to a form. Rifle low and ready, her steps were silent, her silhouette slicing through the alternating red and steady blue.

And then, the Father.

His place is always closest to the threat.

His pace matched their run, relaxed but deliberate, eyes focused and darting. Every corner, every shadow, every flicker of light, measured and assessed.

Something was wrong.

They should have been further by now.

There was no sound to warn him, no shadow on the wall, only the knowing.

He glanced over his shoulder, almost halfway to the next bend. The red pulse stretched the moment, and in it, a shapeless blur appeared.

The Last Bridge

A black mass slammed into the far wall, behind at the last hallway bend, rebounding without losing speed. Not from clumsiness, this was acceleration at its limit.

Claws scraped stone, throwing sparks. A Hellhound, chest high and ripping lean muscle, churned forward in a blur of motion. Blue light sliced its shape into jagged shadows; the red crowned its back in a halo of blood light.

The Father kept his stride a heartbeat longer, eyes locked on the wave of black snarling anger closing the distance.

A second Hellhound exploded from the bend behind the first, claws sparking as it skidded for traction.

Then came the Demon Warriors, three of them, flowing around the corner and into a dead sprint, their thin black frames glided with inhuman speed.

The Father slid, pivoting on one heel. His short sword was already drawn, his weight settling into the stance as he came to a full stop, just before the first Hellhound was airborne.

Blue light washed over its matted black fur while in mid leap.

Red light pulsed on.

Steel flashed.

One high arc, through fur, flesh, and bone. The head sailed forward; the body crumpled. Blood sprayed the wall, beading on the glowing blue strip.

The red light faded off.

The second Hellhound didn't hesitate. It lunged over its dead packmate, mouth open, claws cutting the air. The Father twisted low, dragging the blade in a downward slash as he rose. The steel carved across the back of the neck, another spray, a body sailing in the air, another head hitting stone.

The Demon Warriors closed in quickly.

The Father pivoted to meet the first, adjusting his stance to bait its strike.

It lunged, one arm pulling back to skewer him.

He shifted, just enough. A half step, a tilt of his head, slipping out of her line of sight.

Pop. Pop.. Pop.

Suppressor fire cracked from the far end of the hall.

A flash of yellow. Three perfect hits.

First: headshot. Skull snapped back, body folding.

Second: A round through the sternum, spine snapping as it fell.

Third: tried to veer, but didn't make it, the hit sending it sliding lifeless across the floor.

The Father was already turning before the third body hit stone. No nod. No thanks. Just movement.

The Mother pivoted on her toes, rifle lowering without a pause, taking off in a sprint. Moving to the next bend at full speed.

The children had already vanished ahead.

She rounded the bend to a heavy wooden door that stood waiting and open. Without breaking stride, she caught the handle, spun and pushed. Bracing off the wall, throwing her full weight into it. Forcing it to give. Slowly yielding to close.

The Father slipped through the narrowing gap like a shadow.

SLAM.

The door coming to rest into its new position.

He grabbed the locking bar from its mount, yanking it up and over.

The Mother ducked under his arm, already moving at full speed, following the children, still out of view.

CLANG.

Bar dropped into its locking place.

They were running again, side by side now. Equal pace.

The children appeared ahead, tight formation. Alive.

No chatter.

No hesitation.

Just forward.

Toward the light growing at the end of the tunnel.

Chapter Seven: The Line We Draw

When making a stand is the only way forward.

The family spilled from the tunnel into open light.

A small, sloped outcrop of half matted grass and weeds led straight to the start of a narrow bridge. Made from large ancient stone, a relic from another age.

It stretched away for what looked like a thousand meters or more, suspended over a drop so deep the mist never rose high enough to reveal the bottom.

Wind howled through the gap like the voice of something that had been waiting centuries.

Ahead: sheer cliffs, with a trail cut into the rock, tight switchbacks barely wide enough for a single person. The only escape.

Behind: death without mercy.

And behind that death... something worse.

They moved fast.

Not wild. Not panicked.

Tactical. With the urgency of purpose.

At point: The Eldest, the sniper, recon and fastest.

Left flank: The Son, the heavy gunner, payload of promise and presence.

Right flank: The Youngest, the medic, light quick and able.

Center control: The Mother, the tactician, rifle low, muzzle steady, her trigger finger on the receiver, it's only safety.

Rear guard: Father, four steps behind, the highest lethality closest to threat, weapons that were part of him. No need for reloading, no controlled rate, no cooling, just needs to be released to kill.

Always closest to the threat is his position.

He measured the distance to the far cliff face, then glanced back to confirm his math.

His expression was steady, carved in certainty.

His pace slowed.

Eight paces behind.

Sixteen.

The Last Bridge

Thirty two, midstride, he stopped.

No whisper of an order. No indication of a change to their battleplan.

Just boots planted on ancient stone, back straight, eyes locked on the four figures still running.

One. Two. Three. Four.

All still moving.

All still breathing.

He watched them like a man burning their image into memory.

The Mother felt it before she saw it.

Thirty meters ahead, she looked back.

And he wasn't at his location.

She stopped. Turned.

He had not fallen, was not wounded.

Just planted standing and still.

Watching them go.

Her breath caught. The truth hit a heartbeat later.

This wasn't hesitation.

It was clear intent.

Their eyes locked across the span.

She took a step toward him.

His hand rose; fist closed.

Command: Hold.

The hand flattened; pulling back slightly.

Command: Fall back.

She knew that signal. She'd taught it to the kids herself.

To move on to safety and not look back.

It was meant for them together. They would hold off a crushing threat allowing the children to escape.

But she had never seen him use it.

The meaning hitting her in the chest.

Her jaw tightened. Her boots planted.

Hand letting go of the forward grip of her weapon, moving to a small cylinder strapped to her chest rig.

Light in weight, crushing in meaning.

He saw the motion.

Gave a single, confirming nod.

That was all.

She turned back toward their children, their hope.

And ran.

Ran with everything she had.

She had to get in position.

He turned too, back toward the towering castle walls.

Facing the hallway pulsating with an illumination of an immediate threat.

Faint blue glow and slow, deliberate red pulses still marked the tunnel beyond.

He walked toward it, unhurried.

From the deep, shadows inside bubbled like boiling tar, swelling to the ceiling.

He kept walking.

Drew both blades, one long, one short.

Exhale controlled. Gaze sharp. Clear and Focused.

Stopped a few meters from the beginning of the narrow bridge.

Left foot forward, right back. The balls of his feet holding his weight perfectly balanced with his knees slightly bent. His stance set and ready.

The black tide broke.

A wave of Demon Warriors and Hellhounds poured into the out crop clearing, swarming, clawing, snarling to be the first to reach him.

His grip tightened.

He stood his ground.

The Last Bridge

And waiting on which unlucky creature would be the first to die.

Chapter Eight: The Flood Breaks

When the tide doesn't rise, it erupts.

The first unlucky creature was a Hellhound, foam laced jaws snapping for his throat.

The long sword met it in midair, severing the head in a single, clean arc.

Then the rest poured through.

Four.

Eight.

More.

Snarling. Sprinting.

Claws tearing gouges into ancient stone.

Patchy black fur, awkwardly stretched over bone, and lean muscle. Its eyes hard locked on, desperation driving every step.

The Father moved.

No hesitation. No waste.

The Last Bridge

Arms and blades cut in blinding arcs, head and shoulders slipping just out of reach, feet gliding across the stone with the control of a dancer and the edge of a scalpel.

Short sword swept low to the right, two legs gone from a bounding Hellhound.

Long sword came high to the left, clean through the neck of a lunging Demon Warrior.

Pivot back to the right, short blade through the legless Hellhound's skull before it hit the ground.

Long sword dropped, took the next Hellhound down its length, splitting it clean, while it jumped from the side. Tried to surprise from the flank, only the surprise frozen on each separate half of its face.

He pivoted. Sidestepped. Spun.

Blades flashed like lightning.

Bodies fell like anchors.

Some died in the air, others while sprinting. None got close.

Hellhounds crashed at his boots, limbs twitching, steam curling from split bellies onto cold stone.

More Demon Warriors followed.

Lithe, skeletal, black skinned Demon Warriors with limbs too long, jaws too wide, claws like needles. They crawled over their dead and skittered along the high stone railing. Maneuvering to dive from above, and leap in from the sides.

He met them as if swatting oversized, venomous insects.

Long sword to open.

Short sword to finish.

Short blade to cripple.

Long blade to end.

One went low; he stomped down. Its clavicle snapped while its trachea collapsed under his boot.

Another came high; his arm flying. Short sword punched up through the mouth, twist, withdrawing in one smooth motion.

Hot sticky black blood had coated his face, arms and chest.

Still more came.

The Last Bridge

He held.

Four Demon Warriors moved in, adjusting attack tactics.

Two on the left, one on the right, one just behind.

He read them before they moved.

Stepping forward, the long sword sheared a torso clean through.

Rotate. Now only three at his back; following the long swords swing, as it slices across the length of his back. Part of an arm and half a jaw falls.

Rotated all the way around, facing the remaining two; short sword ready for the one in mid leap from behind. A clean vertical cut split it in two.

Dropping low, the long sword thrust forward, disappearing into the last one; its face showing its confusion on what just happened, its lunge halted.

No time to gather or celebrate as the next came at him. Then the next and the next. No breaks to the Hellhounds and Demon Warriors relentlessly throwing themselves at him. One out of fifty might score a scratch here and hard strike there. It was the only success they could score against him before they died.

Not an inch back.

Not a single break in his line.

Breathing steady.

Mind three seconds ahead.

A Brute tried to force itself into the bottleneck deep in the corridor.

Its roar rolled down the walls like thunder.

Too big to fit.

The Father didn't flinch, only let the corner of his blood splattered mouth curl into a satisfied grin.

Two seconds: Target one. Hellhound

Five meters: Target two. Demon Warrior

Short sword drove deep, dropping under the backswing, pivoted, long blade came up; two targets died standing.

They collapsed backward into the wave behind them, adding to his wall of corpses.

The Last Bridge

The frenzied horde on the other side was climbing, tripping, and falling off the sides into the void. Screaming and howling out of anger as they rained down into the nothingness below.

Desperately pushing up and over. An unorganized attack of blind rage, they kept coming at him. The dead slowing the crushing tide to a trickle, each one dying in turn and adding to the pile.

Their attempts come to a pause.

Just short enough to hear their blood drip from his blades.

Enough to feel his heartbeat in his teeth.

And enough for something far worse to arrive.

An explosion breaks the moment.

Three meters above the hallway entrance, the castle wall erupts outward.

Stone flies through the air. Dust rains down.

Brutes, too large for the hallway, made their own door.

Eight feet of muscle plated in bone bound armor, each dragging a bludgeoned chunk of shard steel. Most streaked with the dried blood from poor victims, unlucky enough to cross his path.

And behind them, dozens. Hundreds. Scores.

Hellhounds. Demon Warriors. Brutes.

The tide was not receding.

It was cresting to crash over.

He slid his foot back, committed to holding the line. Not one inch would be given.

Reversing the long sword, blade down.

Raising the short sword tip out.

Ready.

The stone wall had not stopped them.

The wall of the dead wouldn't.

But he would.

A quick twist and shake of the long blade flung the black blood from its edge.

His grip tightened.

The Last Bridge

His stance locked.

He is the unbreakable wall that will hold them back.

Chapter Nine: Set and Ready

When holding the line is their only way out.

The Brute dropped from its punched out perch, hitting the ground with a thunderous quake.

Both hands gripped its oversized cleaver, swinging it overhead as it charged roaring, desperate to split him in two.

The Father stood alone, just on the other side of his corpse wall.

Holding the line.

The Brute's stumbling unsteady run closed the distance to the makeshift wall of the dead.

The Hellhounds and Demon Warriors, maneuvering for their attacks, ended up scrambling out of the Brute's way, for their own survival. It stepped on, smashed through them with no thought.

Crashed through the corpse wall sending the bodies flying.

The Father sheathed the long sword.

Drew his pistol from his right hip.

The Last Bridge

One exploding round blew its knee apart in a spray of bone and meat.

It howled in pain, cleaver clattering to the ground as both hands clutched the ruin of its leg.

The Father's left hand brought the short sword up and drove it under the Brute's jaw.

Its expression frozen, a state of shock, it slumped forward, plugging the breach with its own body.

The Father holstered in the same motion, pulled his long sword free, and went back to work cutting down those who started to flow over the Brutes back.

He may have stood alone.

But he knew that he wasn't unprotected.

On the far side of the chasm, the high cliff wall rose like a fortress.

The Eldest had led them there.

Her first mission: to get them to safety; now done.

The second: unspoken, but clear.

She pivoted, and no longer holding back her speed, the instant they reached solid ground.

She sprinted up the switchback trail in a blink. Needing elevation. Her rifle, already in hand. Dropping behind a jagged rise.

No wasted movement. No hesitation.

Braced her rifle on the outcrop of a rock.

Cheek touched the stock, finger depressing…

CRACK.

A round split the void.

It punched through a charging Brute's eye socket.

Reverberating an echo then announces her presence on the battlefield.

The beast toppled sideways into a knot of Demon Warriors, crushing three beneath it.

The Father didn't look up. He didn't need to.

Her shot told him what he needed to know.

They were safe.

Her primary mission: Complete.

Secondary: Being executed time now.

Now he only needed to fight his way back. Too easy.

He spun, long sword back in hand, cutting a Demon Warrior from mid air.

The short blade followed low and horizontal. Catching another across the ribs.

Two fell. Six more surged.

Down the slope, the Son slammed his SAW into position across a rock ledge.

Bipod down. Charging handle racked.

He sighted on the hallway mouth and unleashed a stream of burning tracers.

THUD-THUD-THUD-THUD.
THUD-THUD-THUD-THUD.
THUD-THUD-THUD-THUD.

Short, controlled, pinpoint burst of fire echoed.

The light of the tracers punching through lines of enemies, they become sprinting bodies as they fell. The light from the tracers casting twisting blinking strobes of shadows against the walls.

Demon Warriors and Hellhounds dropped in clusters. The flow slowed but never stopped.

The dead being shoved to the side, stepped on or over. Cascading bodies flowed into the void of the chasm. The dead or wounded would take another with it. The horde never took a pause to the vast numbers that has fallen.

A Brute, moved in, staggering through, towering over the rest.

CRACK.

The Eldest's rifle struck again, dropping it mid step. The body toppled into another, sending both off the edge into the abyss.

The Mother fired, controlled and steady rate, one round per target, each finding its mark.

No wasted shots. No hesitation.

The Youngest crouched at the center, hands locked on her med pack.

She didn't fire, that was not her mission.

She watched.

Tracked wounds. Reading her father's rhythm. He was still good. Everything minor and superficial.

Next to the Father, on the ground, a twitch, barely noticeable.

A Demon Warrior lurched itself from the corpse pile, half-dead but still lethal.

Its clawed hand with its four long talons, punched clean through his thigh.

He grunted, staggering half a step.

Mouth wide, turning its head, pulling itself up by the same leg it was stuck in. Desperately trying to bite down.

The long sword came down, severing the arm at the wrist.

The short sword ended it with a single cut through the neck.

The body dropped, headless and armless.

But the hand was still in his leg, its long claws buried deep as it twitched.

He stumbled, recovering.

Sheathing the long sword, pulling out his pistol, and taking aim at a closing Brute.

Across the chasm, the Youngest half rose, eyes locked on the wound, ready to run.

But the Mother's hand clamped her shoulder.

Not yet.

The Eldest's rifle cracked again as two Brutes fell. She aimed just off her father's shot. Timed perfectly to collapse them both, creating a second wall.

The Son's SAW sent a hose of tracers just over the newly formed wall.

The Mother kept her rhythm, three more controlled bursts, then a smooth reload.

Their fire formed a wall thirty meters in front of him.

Their danger close, suppressive fire giving him a lull. Using it to holster, reach down, and rip the severed claw from his thigh.

Dropped it at his feet like trash.

The frothy curdled blood oozed out, soaking down his pant leg.

His blood hopefully pushing out most of the venom.

Pressing the hilt of the short sword to the open wound. Instinct, not treatment.

He is upright. Still moving.

And that means there is still hope.

He only needs to make it to his eager Youngest.

The medic who is already prepping everything he needs. Treat, patch, and ready to move.

He has only one slim chance.

That's all he needs. They have done more with less before.

Drop a small little gift and exfil now. Reach the other side under their cover before rounds run out.

He reached into a small pouch at his side, pulled a short metal tube, and dropped it into the corpse pile beside him.

One of two, set and lying in wait.

Drew his pistol. Hobbled back.

The horde slowed to a stop under the family's disciplined rotation. Two firing, one reloading, then switching without a break. A constant rate of cover.

He moved slowly but steady back. Back to his family, each step a victory.

The few that made it through the families suppressive fire, he dropped easily with a single well placed round.

Two more steps. Another put down.

His pistol locks to the rear.

Empty.

Hit eject, flick to clear out magazine.

Holster. Pull full magazine. Reload.

The Last Bridge

Short sword still in his grip, its hilt pressed against his bleeding leg.

Pistol back in hand, slide released.

An unnerving silence creeps in over the raging battlefield. Fading out the massive volley of fire that is putting up his blocking force.

The horde freezing in mid movement.

They are no longer pushing forward.

The family ceased fire. Holding to assess what has made the horde stop.

A red mist seeps out of the breach in the broken wall.

An unnatural sound followed. Deep, slow, deliberate.

A low rolling base hitting the ground.

This was something that was shear mass moving.

Each strike made the air grow heavier.

The world tilted.

The real enemy was coming.

Stopping his movement to safety.

The Father was not going to lead this to his family.

He straightened.

Slid the short sword home.

Keeping the leg pistol, drawing the second from the chest rig.

Blood pooled at his boot.

But his stance was steady.

Ready.

Chapter Ten: The Demon Lord
When power doesn't wear a crown, it has horns.

The horde tide has broken.

It has come to a full stop.

All for this descending sound in the mist.

Not for reverence or obedience.

Not just from fear. From pure terror.

The remaining Hellhounds slunk backward, heads low, tails curled between their legs.

Demon Warriors crouching away trying to escape to the shadows, limbs drawn tight, to guard themselves.

Brutes hung their heads giving way. One, trembling, took a wrong step and plunged silently into the chasm. Being too terrified to scream, as to not anger its master as it died.

Across the void, the family held their fire.

Out of wonder, not mercy.
Their barrels letting out low tinking sounds, shedding off extreme heat.

As their weapons hold steady on targets in their hands.

No one moved.

No one breathed.

The air thickened, heavy with anticipation.

Cobblestones shivered. Once... twice... long pauses between each impact.

Something huge.

Something deliberate.

The red mist deepened, oily, alive.

Then a hoof landed.

Black. Cracked. The size of a bolder.

It struck stone with the sound of a war drum.

Another followed.

Massive. Crimson furred trunks of muscle rippled with each step.

The Last Bridge

It emerged from the breach in the wall, its shadow spilling forward like a living tide.

And the world felt smaller.

It wore no armor. Needed none.

A ragged brown loincloth hung low over its hips.

Its torso was a wall, with shoulders and chest carved from living iron, skin a deep crimson.

Arms like siege towers swung at its sides, each hand the size of a man's chest, fingers tipped with black nails sharp as daggers.

And above that impossible frame…

A face.

Almost human,

But stretched, warped and twisted wrong.

The jaw too long. The brow too wide. The mouth… too full of teeth.

From its skull rose two massive horns. Each four feet in length and ten inches thick at the base.

Black. Curved. Ancient.

A menacing tower at twelve feet.

This was no beast.

This was dominion.

The Demon Lord.

It stood alone because it needed nothing else.

Behind it, the red mist pulsed in time with something not quite breathing.

The Father didn't move.

Blood streamed from his thigh in a thin, steady line. His skin was mapped in fresh cuts and bruises, but his gaze was locked and unshaken.

He stood in the center of the bridge, alone. Bleeding. Calm.

Two pistols loose in his hands.

The Demon Lord advanced.

Not fast.

The Last Bridge

It didn't need speed.

It descended with purpose, that it was inevitable.

It was endless, and time had no meaning to it as it closed in.

On the far side, the family held position.

The Youngest's knuckles whitened around her med pack.

The Son slammed a fresh belt home, barrel on his SAW glowing faint yellow.

The Eldest never left her scope.

The Mother lowered her rifle just enough to see clearly with her own eyes.

None fired.

Not yet.

They waited, measuring the moment.

Setting the trap. Holding for the signal.

The Demon Lord walking over its dead.

With no concern, they lie there with no value.

Its faithful army crunching under each massive hoof fall.

Walking through the wall of corpses like a spiderweb.

Stopping twenty meters away.

It looks down and laughs. A deep low roll vibrates through every stone.

"It's but a boy," it says mockingly.

Its voice like gravel in a hurricane.

The Father's only reply, direct and immediate action.

His arms flashed up, both pistols thundering, explosive tipped rounds hammering center mass. Signal given.

From the other side, every weapon let loose, a full volley, every round hitting its mark.

The Father held his pistols in position, slides locked back, smoke curling from the barrels and empty breaches.

No effects on target.

The Demon Lord let out a thunderous laugh, so deep and rolling, it swallowed up the furious storm of gunfire still crashing against it.

SAW, sniper, carbine. Every round struck true. None broke the skin.

The Mother's hand cutting the air in front of her face.

Command of: Cease fire! Cease fire!

The guns went silent, barrels hissing.

The Father did not wait and surged forward. Faster than his wounds should allow, closing the gap in five pounding strides.

His guns fell, as both swords came free. Slash low. Spin. Slash high.

The Demon Lord's laugh ended but not his smile. That remained mockingly.

It blocked without effort, using only its hands.

It caught the steel blades between its claws, its movements precise and ancient, as if it had authored the art of killing men like him.

The Father pressed harder.

Strike. Turn. Feint. Real strike.

The long sword struck, embedding itself deep into the left horn.

It was stuck.

The Demon Lord's smirk vanished. It moved, far too fast to track.

One massive hand smashed the short sword from the Father's grip, sending it clattering across stone. While the other clamped onto his right arm, wrist to bicep, disappeared in a crushing grip.

The Father was lifted clean off the bridge.

Boots dangled above the stone.

Blood dripped from his leg. His lip was split open. His chest heaved in labored bursts.

But his eyes stayed locked forward.

The Demon Lord raised him high, bringing him face to face.

Its breath washed over him: rot, sulfur, and death.

The Last Bridge

His free hand reaches to the small of his back, pulling a knife free.

He slashes, hitting true, as his blade open a deep line across its cheek.

The Demon Lord's eyes slammed shut with a wince.

It jerked its head back and lifted him higher. Its massive hand crushing down.

Pain shot through his arm as it splintered. His grip faltered for a moment on his knife.

He swung again, but too wide, too far.

The Demon Lord's eyes snapped open, burning with rage.

A massive backhand smashed across his face, spraying blood in an arc over the bridge.

The knife slipped free, tumbling to the stone with a dull, defeated clatter.

On the far side, the family watched.

The Eldest eased her cheek from the rifle stock.

The Son stood as his SAW barrel smoked, belt empty.

The Youngest trembled, one foot forward, unable to move.

The Mother's gaze never wavered.

Her hand slid free of her forward grip.

Moving with purpose to the cylinder on her chest rig.

The one they'd agreed on.

The Father took stock.

Weapons: Empty, missing, out of reach.

Face: Broken, bleeding, jaw loose, one good eye.

Arm: Crushed, useless.

Leg: Barely leaking now, not enough blood left, venom absorbed.

	He turned his head over his suspended arm, forcing his one good eye to search for them.

He was just able to make them out.

All of them.

The Last Bridge

Standing. Watching. Holding the line for him as he had for them.

His reason for living is safe. That's all that matters.

Just one last thing left to set his mind at ease.

One last look, long enough to remember.

Then back to work, back to the Demon Lord.

Its face full of rage, kissed with a fresh cut line.

It swung the Father back in close, now unarmed and helpless.

It wanted to gloat, strait to his face.

The Father let a curve of a smile lose.

It spread out, bigger than his battered mouth could manage.

Slowly his arm rose, cutting the narrow gap between them.

Breaking into view was a finger slowly ascending.

His fully extended middle finger, inches from the Demon Lords face.

Pulling up as much as he could from the back of his throat.

His broken mouth spat out a dark red thick spray striking the Demon Lord's eye.

It flinched.
Letting loose a deafening roar.

The bridge, walls, and even the air shook.

A hurricane of hot, rotten breath blasted into his face.

Streaking his blood back across his cheeks.

The Father didn't flinch.

His one good eye and smile flapping from the hot rotten windstorm bellowing across his face.

This Demon Lord wasn't going to break him or his line.

He will never be done fighting. His full strength was never used.

The Demon Lord, blind to the love that had his back.

With that there will always be hope.

The Last Bridge

Because of what they have, they will never be defeated.

Behind him, the family stood their ground steadfast.

Pride and defiance carved into their faces.

The Mother's hand tightened on the cylinder.

Her eyes held steady.

The cap snapped open.

Her lips pressed tight.

The trigger was bare.

Tears welled but didn't fall.

But her thumb did.

Chapter Eleven: Ashes and Sunlight
When sacrifice carves the way forward.

The far side of the bridge vanished, just a bright spark of light.

Not fire at first.

Pressure, that built in silents, growing and blinding.

Then the sound.

A single, shattering pulse.

Then the heat.

The explosion punched outward from the Father's position without warning, without grace.

A contained microburst. It was directional and absolute.

It enveloped everything.

Hellhounds. Demon Warriors. Brutes.

The Demon Lord itself.

All swallowed in a sphere of annihilation.

The Last Bridge

Their screams never made it past their teeth.

Steel vaporized.

Stone turned to dust.

The bridge buckled with a wave, then collapsed.

Chunks of carved stone plummeted into the chasm trailing smoke, blood, and bone.

The Demon Lord didn't go flying off. Like some of the other bodies, that rained out.

It didn't fall into the void.

No parts could be seen burning.

It was just, gone.

The wave blasted against the cliff's edge where the family stood.

Not close enough to harm. Close enough to shake their stance.

He was gone.

No one spoke.

They didn't kneel.

They stood there

The remaining four.

Holding, out of reverence and honor.

The Eldest raised her rifle, scanning rapidly through the falling debris.

Maybe for hope, maybe for confirmation, or maybe to put one last round through something needing to die at her hand. Her finger never twitched.

The Son's grip slackened, sling biting into his shoulder as the SAW's glowing barrel cooled.

The Youngest let her med pack drop, one hand covering her mouth.

The Mother…

She kept her eyes fixed, focused on empty air. Where her love was last seen.

It is not out of disbelief. Nor from fear she held onto the spot.

The Last Bridge

It was to take a split second longer before letting go of the past, and the new reality taken in.

Her hand slid down, the spent detonator in her palm, going limp to her thigh before hanging at her side. The welled tears still held, unwilling to let them, or him go.

Not yet.

Out of pride and out of honor she let her tears fall.

Not out of grief, that will be later.

The wind rose, carrying ash into the sky like light gray snow.

The bridge was gone. So was the enemy.

So was he.

Her husband, their father had done it.

No last words. No hero's flourish.

Just strategy. A sacrifice and execution of only what was needed.

The way forward was safe.

Smoke drifted, not thick, not choking, just… present. The kind that lingers after something important ends.

They stood at the cliff's edge a moment longer, then the Eldest stepped off first.

One foot, then another, up the narrow trail carved into the cliff face. Rifle returned to it spot, tight across her back. Eyes shimmering with tears from what she had witnessed. Pain and pride stamped on her face. She will guard his legacy and his sacrifice.

The Son turned and followed. Bandolier empty. Barrel cool. No longer the boy, but pushed into a new position. A new roll and responsibilities. He will carry it, as he must. He can no longer just be the massive firepower. He must become a weapon with purpose. For him, for them, he will.

The Youngest adjusted her pack. No trembling now. She walked. Because he would expect it. She would never let his pain be theirs or hers. She will be strong, for him, like him, and in honor of him.

The Mother lingered last.

Her gaze swept the wreckage, not searching, just acknowledging.

The Last Bridge

She held the cylinder tight in her hand, nodded once. She let it go, falling to the ground.

For him, this will be his grave marker. She knew he would like that and expected nothing more.

The path rose in switchbacks, sky opening above.

Clouds broke.

Sunlight fell in long golden bands across the stone.

They climbed up, up into the casting light.

No fanfare.

No music.

Just boots on rock, dust in their lungs, and the weight of everything he gave them etched into every step.

They were alive.

Together.

And because of him;

They were not done.

Epilogue: The Line Holds

The bridges we cross.

There are many chasms we face.

There are moments when the air turns and the ground shakes beneath us.

But for this family, on this day, they stood together, against death itself.

It was paid for. The price was in blood and pain, with the last breath of a father who refused to give an inch. He bought hope for what he loved.

Their path ahead would be narrow, steep, and unforgiving. Even more so without him.

It didn't matter.

They would make it.

They would walk it.

Always forward.

Always together.

They would climb out.

The Last Bridge

Not for him. Because of him.

He will always be part of them, his sacrifice, his training, his rules, his line.

They were theirs now.

And they would hold it, just as fiercely as he did.

At this moment of peace, they would carry it,
rare and priceless as an answered prayer.

Father's Rules

1. Family is all that matters.

2. Protect what matters with every action.

3. Breathe, steady and true.

4. Choose a line. Everyone holds it.

5. Fear is a weapon. Never hand it to the enemy.

6. Bleed if you must, but never stop moving.

7. Stand until you can't.

8. When you can't, make your last stand count.

9. Always forward, no matter what.

10. Only look back to check, never for a place to go.

About the Author

Ronan Valehart is, first and always, a hard working father and husband. Then a Soldier who served with distinction for his country with pride from 1998 until retirement in 2025. Across more than two decades of service, he traveled to over ten countries and twenty seven U.S. states, including Alaska and Hawaii, experiencing the full span of cultures, climates, and challenges that shaped his perspective on life and resilience.

His career carried him through multiple combat deployments in several theaters, leadership roles, and the kind of moments that leave their mark far beyond the battlefield. This story was born from the quiet hours of recovery during medical treatment for service related traumatic brain injury. A testament to the healing power of storytelling and the human need to create, even in the shadow of hardship.

Off duty, Ronan is a motorcycle enthusiast, a homebody at heart that is building or tinkering on something, and someone who finds his greatest joy in the company of his family most of all. He continues to explore new ventures, often working alongside creative collectives like AmeraVinci Ventures, whose mission is to bring unique, powerful voices and creations into the world.

For Ronan, every story is more than words on a page, it's a way to honor the past, protect the present, and light the way forward. He prays that his simple words might reach those who need it. To give a glimpse towards hope, to provide that little bit of something. That it might provide someone, just enough to start to climb out of their hurt and out of their darkness. Knowing that you are never truly alone. Others may have given everything, and to honor them, is why we need to fight our way out and climb.

www.ingramcontent.com/pod-product-compliance
Lightning Source LLC
Chambersburg PA
CBHW030539180626
46810CB00005B/1938